DON'T GET CAUGHT WEARING THE LUNCH LADY'S HAIRNET

Other books by Todd Strasser

DON'T GET CAUGHT WEARING THE LUNCH LADY'S HAIRNET

TODD STRASSER

AN
APPLE
PAPERBACK

SCHOLASTIC INC.

New York Toronto London Auckland Sydney
Mexico City New Delhi Hong Kong

ISBN 0-439-21063-1

12 11 10 9 8 7 6 5 4 3 2 1   1 2 3 4 5 6/0

Printed in the U.S.A.   40

First Scholastic printing, January 2001

*To Fred, Deb, Julia, Maddy,
and Lucky because they showed
how much they cared. And
because Lucky shared her hot dogs.*

DON'T GET CAUGHT WEARING THE LUNCH LADY'S HAIRNET

Hey, I'm Kyle Brawley. As you may know, I'm the kid who got busted for driving the school bus. And if you didn't know that, I'm still that kid.

I'm in seventh grade, and it wasn't like I took the bus for a joyride. I *had* to drive it or we would have had a major 911 complete with Medivacs and TRAIN SMEARS SCHOOL BUS–type headlines.

Of course, that didn't stop Principal Monkey Breath (his real name is Chump) from trying to seriously nail me and my best buds Wilson Kriss and Dusty Lane. He came pretty close, but my friends and I managed to slip through his sticky fingers.

Anyway, that happened a couple of months ago so it's pretty much history now. I promised my mom and Principal Chump and just about everyone else in the world that I wouldn't get into any more trouble.

But then this thing came up with the Psycho Lunch Monitors from H.E.L.L. And that changed everything.

What can I say? Sometimes a guy's got to do what a guy's got to do.

"Good morning. You're watching Hart TV and I'm your host, Gary Gordon."

"And I'm Alice Appleford."

It was homeroom period at Hard Marks Middle School and Gary and Alice were on the school TV. Every morning we were supposed to watch the five-minute news show hosted by the two biggest butt oxen in school. It had to be the longest five minutes of the day.

Alice is our class president. She has straight, shoulder-length blond hair that is always perfect and she usually wears skirts to school and sometimes even dresses. She wears glasses even though Wilson says there's nothing wrong with her eyes. He says she wears them because she thinks they make her look smart.

Gary Gordon is the class secretary and the editor of the yearbook. He has longish hair that he parts in the middle, and his eyes are always bloodshot and teary because he really does need

3

glasses, but he insists on wearing contact lenses instead.

As usual, the *Gary and Alice Show* was all about school events and public service junk. No one in our homeroom was paying attention. Even Ms. Taylor, our homeroom and science teacher, was using the time to mark papers.

The scene on the TV shifted to the school cafeteria. Our friend Melody Autumn Sunshine was holding a microphone and standing beside a large brown cardboard box. Painted on the box in big green letters was:

RECYCLE AND WIN!

Melody's parents are hippies, so she tends to wear her brown hair long and braided. She has green eyes and a relaxed smile. And she wears beads and lots of silver rings on her fingers.

"As you can see, the recycling committee has placed this big cardboard box in the cafeteria," Melody said.

"Now *that's* really exciting," Dusty groaned in his seat next to mine. Like I said before, Dusty is one of my two closest friends. He's tall and lanky and easygoing. His nickname is King Calm. (My other close friend is Wilson — but he wasn't in homeroom because he worked behind the scenes at Hart TV.)

"Yeah, really exciting." Cheech the Leech

groaned and pretended to be bored because that's what Dusty had done. Cheech isn't a bad kid; he just doesn't know what he is. So each day he morphs into what he thinks he should be.

What happened next on the TV was actually borderline amusing. Melody turned to the box. "So, Mr. Recycling Box, how does it feel to be at the Hard Marks Middle School?"

She tilted the microphone as if she expected the box to answer.

"It sure beats what I used to do," a voice inside the box replied.

Around homeroom, kids looked up at the TV for the first time all morning. I forgot to mention that Melody is also the class vice president. The only reason Alice Appleford got elected president of our class was because Melody is supersmart and everybody knows that if Alice totally messes everything up, Melody can always fix it.

"This is new," Dusty chuckled as we watched the TV. "No one's ever interviewed a box before."

On the TV, Melody asked Mr. Recycling Box what he used to do.

"I had a dishwasher inside me," Mr. Recycling Box complained. "It was a real drag. All she ever talked about was soap spots."

"But now you'll be full of plastic and cans and bottles," Melody pointed out.

"That's cool," replied the box. "At least I'll be helping the environment."

Melody turned to the camera. "So that's the morning news from the cafeteria. Back to — "

"Excuse me," a voice suddenly said. On the TV we saw a mysterious hand reach into the picture and take the microphone from Melody.

The next thing we knew, Principal Monkey Breath was on the TV. Our principal is short and has dark hair and really big ears. He always wears dark suits and white shirts and a tie because he thinks it makes him look important.

Standing beside Monkey Breath were two stern-looking women wearing dark green uniforms with name patches over their pockets. One woman was big and husky with short blond hair. Her name was Bertha. The other woman was shorter and wider with black hair that fell to her jawline. Her name was Wanda.

Bertha and Wanda were both wearing black baseball caps that said HELPFUL EDUCATIONAL LUNCHES LTD.

Monkey Breath straightened his tie, stared at the camera, and held up the microphone. "Hello, everyone, this is your principal."

"Gee, I thought it was Bart Simpson," Dusty quipped.

"Yeah, Bart Simpson," Cheech said.

"As you know, I have not been happy with your behavior during lunch," Monkey Breath told the school. "The ability to sit quietly and eat in a civilized fashion is one of the hallmarks that separates human beings from our animal relatives. Yet, when I walk into the lunchroom, I feel as if I'm at the zoo."

Just at that moment I happened to yawn and scratch my arm. When I opened my eyes, Cheech was staring at me. Next thing I knew, he squatted on his chair and pretended to scratch himself while making monkey sounds: "Eeh! Eeh! Eeh!"

"That's enough," Ms. Taylor said. Cheech sat down.

"Therefore, I have hired Bertha and Wanda," Monkey Breath went on. "Two professionally trained monitors from a company called Helpful Educational Lunches Limited. They will enforce the rules of the lunchroom. I have given them orders to report each and every violation to me. Let me assure you that my punishments will be swift and sure."

Monkey Breath handed the microphone back to Melody.

"Well, uh, that's the news from the cafeteria," Melody said. "Back to you, Alice and Gary."

The scene on the TV cut back to the news desk.

"You heard it here first," Gary said. "There'll be

new lunch monitors in t̶
going to be keeping a sharp e̶
lations of the rules." He turned t̶
do you think of that, Alice?"

Alice nodded approvingly. "I think it's a̶
cellent step, Gary." Then she turned to the camera. "And don't forget about Mr. Recycling Box,
everyone. If we win the recycling competition,
the whole school will get a trip to Big Splash Wa-
ter Park."

"And that ends today's show," said Gary.

The TV went blank. The kids in our homeroom
started talking or doing last-minute homework.
Sitting next to me, Dusty sighed and shook his
head. "So, Monkey Breath's hired Bertha and
Wanda from Helpful Educational Lunches Limited."

"H-E-L-L," I spelled.

"Huh?"

"Helpful Educational Lunches Limited. Initials
H-E-L-L," I explained.

Dusty drummed his fingers thoughtfully
against the desk. "The Lunch Monitors from
H.E.L.L. are supposed to teach *us* table manners?
What's wrong with this picture?"

"Plenty," I said.

4

If you were wondering what we thought was
wrong with the picture, I will explain. My
friends and I feel that it is our mission to make
Hard Marks Middle School a "normal" place for
kids instead of a maximum security prison,
which is what Monkey Breath thinks it should
be.

What Monkey Breath believes:	What we believe:
1. School should be all work and no play (except recess).	1. School should be mostly fun and some work.
2. Kids must follow millions of rules to stay out of trouble.	2. Kids have the brains to know right from wrong.

After homeroom I didn't see my friends again
until lunch. Usually the upper school 6–8 kids
don't eat lunch with the lower school K–5 kids,

but that week we were on a special testing schedule so we all had to eat together.

At lunchtime I noticed that the cafeteria had a new look. Alice and her crew had hung long green banners from the ceiling urging everyone to participate in the recycling competition. In addition, Mr. Recycling Box was next to the big gray garbage cans where we dumped our leftovers.

I met up with Dusty and Wilson. Wilson is short and compact. He can get a little bit tense sometimes, especially when he thinks we might get caught doing something wrong.

At the entrance to the kitchen, Big Bertha, Lunch Monitor from H.E.L.L., was standing with her hands on her hips making sure the lunch line was orderly.

Just as we got on the end of the line, we ran into Melody.

"Pretty funny interview this morning," I said.

Melody smiled. "Thanks, handsome." She always calls me that.

"Looks like Mr. Recycling Box is a big hit." Wilson pointed at the box. A bunch of single digits were standing around it, trying to get it to talk to them. A single digit is any kid under the age of ten.

"Too bad you couldn't have someone in there all day to answer their questions," I said.

"Gross." Melody wrinkled her nose. "They'd

get covered with sticky plastic and bottles and foil."

"We could rig a remote camera with a microphone to the wall above the box," Wilson said. "Then you could be in the TV station and see who was talking to Mr. Recycling Box, and answer them."

When Wilson says stuff like that, he's not dreaming. Not only does he work in the control room at Hart TV, but he's an inventor and the handiest kid I know. You give him a screwdriver, wire cutters, and electrical tape, and he can do just about anything.

"Like those cameras they have in stores to make sure people don't steal?" I asked.

"Pretty much," said Wilson. "It would definitely be a kick for the single digits."

"And it would help them remember to recycle," Melody realized. "That would be great, Wilson. You really think you could do it?"

"Piece of cake," Wilson said. "The school has a couple of old video cameras they don't use anymore. I'll just borrow one."

"Hey, Melody!" Gary Gordon came toward us. Only he didn't seem to see my friends and me. He cut between Melody and me as if I weren't even there.

"Mr. Recycling Box looks like a big hit," he said. "I definitely think you should talk to him again tomorrow."

12

"I'm planning to," Melody replied.

"You on the lunch line?" Gary asked her with his back to my friends and me.

"No, she's standing here for her health," Dusty cracked.

Gary turned and narrowed his bloodshot eyes at Dusty. Needless to say, we don't like Gary and he doesn't like us.

"Did I ever tell you guys how much I enjoyed seeing you in handcuffs?" he asked, referring to the picture in the local newspaper of my friends and me after we crashed the school bus.

"Hey, don't forget, it turned out we were heroes," said Wilson.

"Yeah, right." Gary smirked.

A deep voice suddenly interrupted us. "No talking!"

It was Big Bertha in her dark green uniform and black HELPFUL EDUCATIONAL LUNCHES LTD. cap. She was carrying a fat white ring binder.

"What?" Dusty asked her.

"No talking on the lunch line," said Bertha.

"But we always talk on the lunch line," I said.

"Not anymore," said Bertha.

"Why not?" Melody asked.

"It slows the line," said Bertha. "When there's no talking you pay more attention. The line moves faster and lunch ends sooner."

"But we don't want lunch to end sooner," Wilson said. "And we should be allowed to talk."

"No." Bertha shook her head.

"Don't you talk when you have lunch?" I asked.

Bertha glared at me. "A troublemaker, huh?" She flipped open the white ring binder. Inside were clear plastic sleeves like a photo album. In

14

each sleeve was a photo of a kid. Bertha thumbed through the binder until she found my picture. "Kyle Brawley?"

"At your service." I bowed.

"Am I in there?" Wilson asked, and reached for the binder, but Bertha slammed it shut.

"No fair!" Wilson complained.

"No talking," Bertha snapped.

"How about whispering?" Dusty asked.

"No!" Bertha grumbled. "Move ahead, you're holding up the line."

"Nice talking to you." Dusty waved as we moved forward into the kitchen.

My friends and I got our lunch trays. Standing in front of us were Burpy and Sneezy, two of the single digits from our bus stop. Sneezy has brown hair and a nose that's always red and dripping. Burpy is a cute little girl who wears plaid dresses and always has bows in her red hair.

"Hey, Burpy, wuz up?" Wilson asked.

"No talking!" This warning didn't come from Big Bertha. It came from Wanda the Widebody, who was standing at the other end of the lunch line near the cash register. She was holding a white ring binder, too.

Burpy looked up at Wilson with big, wide eyes. She didn't say a word.

"Whatcha gonna have for lunch?" Dusty whispered to her.

Burpy shook her head as if she was too frightened to answer.

"What's wrong with you guys?" Gary Gordon hissed. "Why are you talking to those little twerps?"

You could see by the way Gary glanced at Melody that he was trying to impress her.

"They're our friends," Wilson whispered back.

"Can't find any friends your own age?" Gary taunted us.

"Like *you*, Gary?" I asked in a low voice.

"It's like this, Gary," Dusty whispered. "We'd rather be friends with little twerps than big butt oxen."

A couple of the kids in line chuckled and even Melody grinned. Gary's face turned red.

"I said, no talking!" Wanda the Widebody barked again.

Dusty caught my attention and rolled his eyes. We slid our trays down the lunch line rail. On the other side of the counter, the lunch ladies were dishing out lunches. I got a bowl of spaghetti and meatballs and slid my tray down to the cold lunch and dessert area.

When I caught up to Burpy and Sneezy, they were in front of the sandwich rack. Burpy reached in for a sandwich, but instead of putting it on her tray, she held it up to the lunch lady.

"Could you cut the crusts off?" she asked.

"Sure, hon." The lunch lady started to reach for the sandwich.

"No cutting off crusts!" Wanda the Widebody announced.

"Why not?" asked Wilson.

"It slows down the line," replied Wanda the Widebody.

"What if a kid doesn't like the crust?" I asked.

"Too bad," snapped Wanda the Widebody. "And no talking!"

"Here, give me that." Dusty took Burpy's sandwich. Using his white plastic lunch knife, he cut off the crusts.

Wanda the Widebody flipped open her ring binder and looked through the pictures. "Dustin Lane?"

"None other," Dusty replied with a bow.

"Can't I see if I'm in there?" Wilson begged.

"No!" Just like Bertha, Wanda the Widebody snapped the binder shut.

"No fair!" Wilson complained.

"Be quiet and keep the line moving," Wanda the Widebody ordered.

"This is just like jail," Dusty muttered.

"I heard that," said Wanda the Widebody.

"Good," said Dusty.

Out in the lunchroom you could tell something weird was going on. Everyone was eating quietly. Big Bertha was patrolling between the tables with her arms crossed. When she saw my friends and me, she marched over and opened the white binder.

"Kyle Brawley, table three, seat K," she announced. "Dustin Lane, table nine, seat D. Wilson Kriss, table twelve, seat F."

My friends and I looked around in shock. On the wall over each lunch table was a freshly painted number. And seat letters had been painted on the lunch table benches.

"Assigned seating?" Wilson gasped in disbelief.

"No talking!" ordered Big Bertha.

For a second, neither Wilson, nor Dusty, nor I budged. I think we were too stunned to move.

"Get to your seats!" Big Bertha ordered.

Dusty looked up and met the lunch monitor's gaze. "This," he growled, "means war."

The new lunch rules were ridiculous:
No talking.
Sit in your assigned seat.
No getting up without permission.
No slouching. They wanted you to sit up straight.
If you got caught running, you had to walk back and forth five times.
If you got caught littering, you had to pick up five additional pieces of garbage from the floor.
And, finally, the rule that got us all sent to the office.
"What?!!!!!" It began with Wilson's high-pitched cry of disbelief. All around the cafeteria kids looked over at table twelve, seat F, to see what was going on. Wanda the Widebody was standing behind Wilson.
"I said spit it out," ordered Wanda the Widebody.
"Are you serious?" Wilson asked loudly.

"Spit it out," Wanda the Widebody repeated.

"No!" Wilson sat stubbornly at the table, chewing.

"What's the problem?" Big Bertha lumbered over from the other side of the lunchroom.

As soon as Big Bertha went to Wanda the Widebody's aid, Dusty and I automatically went to assist Wilson.

"You two sit down!" Big Bertha ordered as she headed to table twelve where Wilson sat chewing and Wanda the Widebody stood glaring.

Neither Dusty nor I listened. We arrived at Wilson's table just as Wilson swallowed.

"What'd he do?" Big Bertha asked Wanda the Widebody.

"Started his dessert before he finished his vegetables," Wanda the Widebody reported.

"Darn right." Using his plastic fork, Wilson broke off another piece of cake.

"You have to finish your vegetables!" Wanda the Widebody ordered.

"Who says?" I asked.

"Sit down!" Big Bertha yelled at me.

"That's the stupidest thing I've ever heard," said Dusty.

"You're not allowed to talk!" Big Bertha yelled at him.

Wilson put the second piece of cake into his mouth and started to chew.

"That's a clear and intentional violation of the

lunchroom rules!" Wanda the Widebody declared.

"You guys are psycho," said Dusty.

"I told you to sit down and stop talking," Big Bertha yelled.

Dusty and I looked at each other and sat down . . . on the floor.

"Not on the floor!" yelled Big Bertha.

"You said to sit down," I said.

Boooooo! Hisssss! All around the lunchroom kids started booing and jeering. Pieces of cake, fruit salad grapes, and meatballs started flying toward the lunch monitors.

Big Bertha grabbed her radio and pressed it against her cheek. "Principal Chump! This is Bertha in the lunchroom! Code red! We have an emergency!"

My friends and I are no strangers to the school office. We know the routine. Monkey Breath always makes you wait a long time on the bench next to the mailboxes before he calls you into his room. As far as we can tell, he does this for three reasons:

1. He hopes you'll feel embarrassed when kids in the hall pass and see you in the office.
2. He hopes you'll feel humiliated when your teachers come into the office and see you there.
3. He hopes you'll feel nervous and scared while you wait to see him.

That may work with other kids, but it never works with Dusty, rarely works with me, and only sometimes works with Wilson.

"You think we're in trouble?" Wilson asked. He

was hunched over on the bench, gnawing on the skin next to his thumbnail.

"This is ridiculous," Dusty grumbled.

"I know it's ridiculous," said Wilson, "but do you think we're gonna get punished?"

The office door opened and Ms. Ivana Fortune came in. Ms. Fortune is our assistant principal. She has red hair and always wears tight skirts and high heels and bright red lipstick. Dusty insists that Hard Marks is the only school anywhere with a babe for an assistant principal.

Ms. Fortune smiled when she saw us. "Time for a new rule, boys?"

"Too late," I said.

Ms. Fortune's smile turned into a frown. "Don't tell me you were caught breaking an *existing* rule?"

My friends and I nodded. But before we could explain how stupid the existing rule was, the door to Monkey Breath's office opened and our principal waved us in. "Come in, boys."

Inside the evil Dr. Monkey Breath's dungeon, the shades were pulled shut. The only light came from a small desk lamp. We knew Monkey Breath kept the shades drawn because he was worried that people would be able to see into his office.

But today we noticed something new. The walls and ceiling of the office were covered with square gray egg trays.

"What's with the egg tray wallpaper?" Dusty asked as he relaxed into a chair.

"Soundproofing," Monkey Breath replied as he closed the door and came around in front of his desk.

"To muffle the sounds of kids screaming while they're being tortured?" I guessed.

Monkey Breath stopped suddenly. "What have you heard?"

"Uh, nothing," I said.

"None of it's true," said our principal. "The blood was from a nosebleed, understand? No one's being tortured in here, Kyle. I don't know where you kids get those ideas."

Monkey Breath likes to stand when he talks because then he feels like he's towering over us. The trouble when he's that close is we get some pretty fierce whiffs of toxic monkey breath.

"I hear you boys had a problem in the cafeteria," our principal said.

My friends and I shared innocent, puzzled looks.

"It wasn't us, it was the lunch monitors," Dusty said.

"The *psycho* lunch monitors," I added.

"The Psycho Lunch Monitors from H.E.L.L.!" Wilson concluded.

My friends and I slapped palms.

"Enough, boys." Our principal let out another killer blast of toxic monkey breath, then picked up a pink report sheet. "It says here that you were talking."

"We were talking to the psycho lunch monitors," Dusty said.

"The new rules state no talking in the cafeteria," said Monkey Breath.

"But the lunch monitors were talking to us," I said. "Wouldn't it be impolite if we didn't answer?"

Monkey Breath frowned, took out a pen, and jotted something in the margin of the report sheet. "Good point. I suppose we'll have to amend that rule to state that there's no talking unless you are spoken to first. Now, it also says here that Wilson began to eat his dessert before he finished his vegetables."

"No one's ever told me I couldn't," Wilson argued.

"It's logical," Monkey Breath argued back. "You don't have to be told not to yell fire in the middle of an assembly to know it's wrong."

"But isn't it also logical to assume that all the food gets mixed up in your stomach anyway?" I asked.

"Kyle's right," added Dusty. "It's not like the stomach cares what order the food comes in."

"Boys," Monkey Breath said firmly. "There's a reason why we eat dessert last."

My friends and I waited for him to continue, but Monkey Breath stopped talking.

"Yes?" Dusty prompted him.

"You were saying?" I said.

Monkey Breath scratched his head. "I'll speak to the school nutritionist and get back to you on that. Now, in addition, it says that you and Dusty sat down on the cafeteria floor."

"So?" I asked.

Monkey Breath frowned and went behind his desk where he keeps three thick blue binders filled with school rules. He pulled out the one labeled *School and Cafeteria Rules*. Then he sat down at his desk and started to thumb through it.

My friends and I waited. Finally, Monkey Breath let out a big sigh. Monkey Breath's sighs were both good and bad news. The good news was it meant he couldn't find a rule we'd broken. The bad news was that every sigh was another big cloud of toxic monkey butt mouth odor. Sometimes his breath was so bad you almost wished he'd find a rule you'd broken instead.

Monkey Breath pressed a button on his intercom. "Could you please come in, Ms. Fortune?"

A moment later the door opened and Ms. Fortune sauntered in, her red high heels clicking on the floor. She gave my friends and me a wink, as if to say, "See? I *knew* there'd be a new rule today."

"New cafeteria rule, number six hundred eighty-four." Monkey Breath handed her the thick blue binder. *"There will be absolutely no sitting on the floor of the cafeteria."*

I raised my hand. "What about assemblies?"

"Of course," said Monkey Breath. "Thank you, Kyle. Ms. Fortune, please amend the new rule to state, *There will be no sitting on the floor of the cafeteria unless students are specifically ordered to do so."*

"Got it," Ms. Fortune said.

"That will be all," said Monkey Breath.

Ms. Fortune left, but not before giving my friends and me a big smile. The door closed. Monkey Breath placed his hands on his desk and gazed sternly at us.

"It appears that once again you three have managed to escape punishment," he grumbled. "But let this be a warning, boys. You may have gotten away today, but at some point all the rules will be clear and in place. And then you will get caught. And punished."

Usually, when we leave the office, Wilson is just glad to get away without a detention. But today his eyebrows dipped sharply and he had a big frown on his face.

"I am completely ticked," he announced, "about not being allowed to eat dessert whenever I please. That just makes me totally mad."

"What's the big deal?" Dusty asked. "Like Kyle said, it all gets mixed together anyway."

"It's the principle of the thing," Wilson sputtered. "It's unfair and it violates my constitutional rights."

"The right to eat dessert?" I asked with a scowl.

"Freedom of expression," said Wilson. "I'm serious, guys. Most of the time I don't care about Monkey Breath's dumb rules. I mean, if we're not allowed to glue single digits to their bus seats anymore, big deal. I can live with that. But no one, I mean, *no one* takes away my right to eat dessert when I feel like it!"

Dusty and I traded surprised looks. I don't think either of us had ever seen Wilson get so worked up about a dumb rule. He usually just went along with our scams for the fun of it and for the chance to invent something interesting.

"So what do you propose to do?" Dusty asked.

"Simple," answered Wilson. "We send the Psycho Lunch Monitors from H.E.L.L. back to where they came from."

The next morning, the Five Dwarfs paid the daily bus stop tax to Dusty, who then shared it with Wilson and me. The Five Dwarfs are Barfy, Burpy, Sneezy, Farty, and Sleepy, the single digits who use our bus stop.

"One lollipop and three pieces of stale candy corn for each of us," Dusty grumbled, dividing the loot. "This is ridiculous."

"It's the same junk the barber gives me," Wilson complained as he tore the clear plastic wrapper off the lollipop. "Remember when you started the tax, Dusty? We used to get tons of *good* candy."

Dusty turned to the dwarf pod. "Listen, guys, the quality and quantity of the candy you're paying us has seriously dropped. Now, what are we going to do about this?"

The dwarf pod quivered fearfully.

"Come on, guys," Dusty said. "I need some answers."

"Why don't you just leave them alone?" asked Amazing Nature Girl. Her real name is Angela Nelson-Gear and some people call her Angie, but we prefer Amazing Nature Girl. She's a fourth grader with stringy brown hair who's totally into saving whales and other endangered species.

"Butt out," Dusty said. "This isn't your problem."

"Yeah," said Wilson. "They may be single digits, but they're not endangered."

Before we could get any answers from the dwarfs, the school bus pulled up and Grandma opened the door for us. Wilson, Dusty, and I got on the bus and went to our usual seats in the back. The single digits tended to cluster in the front near Grandma, while Amazing Nature Girl sat in the middle.

"How come you weren't on the bus home yesterday?" I asked Wilson after we sat down.

"I'll show you when we get to school," he answered.

"Does it have something to do with getting rid of the Psycho Lunch Ladies from H.E.L.L.?" Dusty asked.

"Better believe it," Wilson said.

A little while later we picked up Melody at her stop. Melody's hair was braided as usual, and she was wearing beads and a flowery hippie shirt. She came down the aisle and smiled at me. "Hi, handsome."

I felt my face turn red. Melody is really pretty, and all the guys in school like her, but I'm the only one she ever calls "handsome."

"Hey, Melody, want to see what I invented last night?" Wilson asked.

"Sure," said Melody.

Wilson opened his backpack and took out a square of plywood about the size of a piece of bread. On one side four straight blades lined the edge of the square. On the other side was a wooden handle.

"What is it?" I asked.

"The Decrustifyer," Wilson said. "With this thing you can do a whole sandwich at once. I even made the blades extra long for really thick sandwiches."

"You made it because those new lunch monitors won't let the lunch ladies cut the crusts anymore, right?" Melody said.

"Right," said Wilson.

Dusty patted him on the shoulder. "You are one scary dude. Is there anything you can't invent or create?"

Wilson beamed proudly. I rubbed his head. "It's a good thing you're on *our* side," I said.

10

"**Y**ou guys want to come down to the TV station?" Wilson asked when we got into school. "You can see the remote camera for Mr. Recycling Box."

"I thought you were going to get rid of the Psycho Lunch Ladies from H.E.L.L.," said Dusty.

"That, too," Wilson replied.

The TV station was actually two separate rooms. One room was the studio where the cameras and bright lights were and where Alice and Gary sat at the news desk every morning. Then there was the control room, which was where Wilson worked. One wall of the control room was filled with little TV monitors, VCRs, and editing machines.

The morning news show was just starting when we got to the control room. Wilson jumped into a swivel chair, pulled on a pair of earphones, and started watching the show on two different monitors. Each monitor was hooked to a different camera.

On the monitors we could see Alice and Gary at the news desk. We could also see them through the window between the control room and the studio. They were both wearing bright green recycling hats.

"So, Gary, how's our recycling competition going?" Alice asked in that fake excited voice they always used when they were on TV.

"Great, Alice," Gary answered. "Now that we've added Mr. Recycling Box to the cafeteria, a lot of the little kids are really getting into the program."

"What does he mean, 'We added Mr. Recycling Box'?" I hissed. "It was Melody's idea."

Wilson swiveled around in his chair. "Gary Gordon never met a good idea he couldn't call his own." He swiveled back to face the monitors. I was really ticked. It was just like Gary to tell everyone he had something to do with Mr. Recycling Box.

Meanwhile, on TV, Alice gushed, "Speaking of Mr. Recycling Box, here's our roving reporter, Melody Autumn Sunshine, with another exciting interview."

Wilson flicked some switches, and two new views appeared on the monitors. One was in color, showing Melody holding a microphone and standing next to Mr. Recycling Box. The other view was black-and-white and sort of fuzzy. It showed Melody and Mr. Recycling Box from above.

Wilson pointed at the black-and-white shot. "That's from the remote camera."

On the color monitor, Melody smiled into the camera. "Hi, this is Melody Autumn Sunshine, and I'm back in the cafeteria this morning with my new friend." She turned to the box. "So, Mr. Recycling Box, yesterday was your first day. How did it go?"

In the control room, Wilson spoke into a microphone. "It was very filling. I couldn't believe how many cans and empty food containers and pieces of aluminum foil I got."

On the TV monitor, it looked like Wilson's answer was coming from Mr. Recycling Box.

"That leads to a question from Mrs. Reed's first-grade class." Melody unfolded a piece of white paper. "They want to know what happens when you get filled up."

"Every night this nice lady named Sam comes along and empties me," Wilson answered. Sam is our school custodian.

Melody unfolded a yellow piece of paper. "Here's a question from Ms. Parker's kindergarten class. What's your favorite TV show?"

"That's easy," said Wilson. "Professional boxing."

Even in the control room, you could hear people groaning at that pun. Meanwhile, Melody turned back to the camera. "You heard him, folks. He's the box that likes boxing. Back to you, Alice and Gary."

Wilson flicked some switches, and Alice and Gary appeared on the TV monitors again.

"Well, Alice, I guess it beats bowling," Gary said.

"Bowling?" Alice scowled.

Gary rolled his eyes and turned back to the camera. "And that's it for today, folks. This is Hart TV, signing off."

Wilson slowly pushed a lever, and all the TV screens except the black-and-white remote camera went blank. He pulled off his headphones.

"I'm impressed by the remote camera," I said, "but I still don't see how that's going to get rid of the lunch monitors."

Before Wilson could reply, the studio door opened and Alice and Gary came out. When Alice saw me, she gave me that big gooey smile. "Hi, Kyle. Are you ready to sign up?"

"For what?" I asked.

"A job. Everyone has to bring in recycling materials, but we'll also need collectors, sorters, and builders."

"Builders?"

"To win the competition we not only have to collect recycling materials, we have to display them in a creative way," Alice explained. "You'd be setting a really good example, Kyle. You know how all the boys look up to you. If we could get you and your friends involved, I'm sure we could win the whole thing. Please?"

"Why does everything in this school have to be a competition?" I asked. "Why can't we just recycle stuff because it's the right thing to do? Why do we have to do it *and* beat everyone else?"

"It's not like *everything's* a competition," Alice replied.

"Get real, Alice," Dusty scoffed. "Our school district must have a dillion contests a year. It's not just sports, either. It's academic stuff like spelling and math and geography. It's hobby stuff like chess and model-building and inventing."

"And don't forget the battle of the bands and cheerleading competitions and art shows," Wilson added.

"See?" I said to Alice. "No matter what we do, they come up with a contest about it."

"I wouldn't be surprised if they have a nose-picking competition someday," Dusty said.

"With a prize for the biggest booger," said Wilson.

"Greenest booger," I said.

"Slimiest," said Dusty.

"Tastiest!" cried Wilson.

Alice planted her hands on her hips and jutted

out her chin. "You're just trying to gross me out and get me to go away. Well, it's not going to work. I'm going to stay right here until Kyle tells me when he's going to sign up."

"I'll think about it," I said.

Alice crossed her arms like she wasn't going to budge. "When, Kyle?"

You may have noticed that Alice can be pretty demanding. Some people would call it pushy, obnoxious, and annoying. Personally, I think she can't help herself. She suffers from an uncontrolled desire to win everything.

"Yesterday," I said.

Alice scowled. "What?"

"I'll think about it yesterday," I said.

Alice stared at me with a big frown. "How can you think about it yesterday?"

"Because if I did, I would know what my answer would be today," I explained.

Alice looked at me like I was crazy.

"It's simple," I said. "If I think about it yesterday, then tomorrow would be today."

Alice's lower lip curled down into a pout. "I think you're making fun of me."

"Honest, I'm not," I said.

Briiiinnngg! The bell rang. It was time to go to our next class.

"That was pretty funny, Kyle," Dusty said as we went down the hall.

"Saying I'll think about it yesterday?" I replied.

"Yeah," said Dusty. "Like maybe we'll take that test two days ago."

"Or maybe I made that videotape tomorrow," said Wilson.

"That reminds me," I said. "You didn't finish telling us your plan."

"Hey, guys." Melody was coming toward us in the hall.

"Hey, Melody," I said. "Another good segment."

"Thanks, handsome."

"Doesn't it tick you off that bonehead Gary implied that he was part of inventing Mr. Recycling Box?" Dusty asked.

"I don't care," she said.

"But he's such a total two-faced, brownnosed, double rump scrubber," said Wilson.

"It doesn't matter," Melody insisted. "The important thing is that it will help get kids to recycle."

You knew that would be Melody's answer. After all, her parents are hippies, and they still believe in all that peace and love stuff.

Briiinnng! The second bell rang. We were now all officially late.

"Gotta skate," Melody said.

Dusty and Wilson started to leave, too.

"Hey, Wilson, wait!" I called. "When are you going to tell us your plan?"

"Lunch," Wilson called back.

At lunch that day the Psycho Lunch Monitors from H.E.L.L. warned us to keep quiet and sit in our assigned seats and not eat our desserts first. Everything seemed to go okay until someone started yelling down at the other end of the cafeteria. The first thing I did was stand up and look over at table nine where Dusty sat. He was there. Then I checked table twelve where Wilson should have been sitting.

He wasn't there.

The shouting was coming from the part of the cafeteria where the single digits sat. That's where Wilson was, chopping the crusts off their sandwiches with the Decrustifyer.

"Stop it!" Big Bertha yelled at him.

"What rule am I breaking?" Wilson shot back.

"You're not allowed to cut the crusts off sandwiches," said Wanda the Widebody.

"And where in the rule book does it say that?"

Wilson asked defiantly as he went up and down the rows of single digits chopping off their crusts.

Big Bertha and Wanda the Widebody frowned. "You're not sitting in your assigned seat."

Wilson stopped chopping crusts and handed the Decrustifyer to one of the single digits. "You guys can use this. When you're finished, give it to someone else."

He stomped back to his assigned seat and sat down. The rest of lunch passed without any more incidents. When we finished eating, the Psycho Lunch Monitors from H.E.L.L. called us table by table to dump our leftovers in the garbage and go outside for recess. They wouldn't even let the single digits talk to Mr. Recycling Box.

Outside, Wilson was on the verge of pitching a fit. "I swear, I'm going to get those monkey butt lunch monitors if it's the last thing I do."

"There's something I don't get," I said. "Why'd you want to cut the crusts off the single digits' sandwiches? You don't even like single digits."

"Yeah, but I like those Psycho Lunch Monitors even less," Wilson said, making a fist. *"One decrustification under God, indivisible, with mayo and ketchup for all."*

"Forget about the single digits," Dusty said. "Tell us your plan already."

"Plan for what?" asked Melody, who'd joined us.

"Plan to get rid of the lunch monitors," I said.

Before Wilson could say a word, Alice came by in her bright green recycling cap. "I've been thinking about what you said, Kyle. You're right. It's not about winning. It's about consciousness-raising."

"What's that?" Wilson asked.

"It's when the daddy consciousness and the mommy consciousness have a little baby consciousness and raise it," Dusty said.

"Like hamsters?" I asked.

Melody laughed.

"Exactly *not*!" Alice got flustered. "Consciousness-raising means making people think about something they haven't thought of before. The reason we want to win this competition is because it will make everyone in school more aware of recycling, and then it will become a regular part of their lives."

"Like brushing after every meal?" I guessed.

"And changing your underwear at least once a week," said Dusty.

"And remembering to put the toilet seat down," said Wilson.

"I thought you're supposed to put the toilet seat up," said Dusty.

"You are," I told him.

"But isn't that the opposite of putting it down?" Dusty asked.

"It depends on the order you do it in," I tried to explain. "First you have to remember to put it up, then you have to remember to put it back down."

"Why?" Dusty asked.

"Because otherwise at night your sister will go into the bathroom and sit down and the seat won't be there," said Melody.

"I don't have a sister," said Dusty. "I have three brothers."

"Then maybe your mother will do it," Wilson said.

Dusty shook his head. "My mom has her own bathroom. She says she'd rather die than set foot in our bathroom."

"Thanks for sharing that with us." Melody winked.

"I don't know about you guys, but I definitely feel like I've had my toilet seat consciousness raised," I said.

"Lowered is more like it," Wilson cracked.

By now Alice's face was red, and she clenched her teeth. "I know you're still trying to gross me out, but it's not going to work. And I'm going to prove to you that I don't just care about winning. I really do care about recycling!"

"Hey, chill," I said. "Just go with the flow."

"Or in this case, the flush," added Dusty.

Alice gave us a major eye roll. "You guys are impossible!"

She turned and stormed away, but I had a feeling she did it mostly so we wouldn't see her smiling.

After Alice left, I turned to Wilson. "For the last time, what's the plan for getting rid of the lunch monitors?"

"The remote camera," Wilson said. "It looks like your basic live feed, but I've leapfrogged it to a voice-activated VCR running an eight-hour loop."

"You don't say," said Dusty.

"I do say," said Wilson.

"Now say it in English," I suggested.

"Oh, come on, guys," Melody said. "All he means is he's hooked it up to record whatever happens during the day."

"We'll check it every day after school," Wilson explained.

"Forget it, partner," said Dusty. "I'm not hanging around here for eight hours after school looking at a tape of kids dumping junk in a box."

"It's voice-activated so it only runs when

someone's talking," Wilson said. "And we'll fast-forward."

"I still don't get it," I said. "How's that going to help us get rid of the Psycho Lunch Monitors from H.E.L.L.?"

Wilson smiled. "You'll find out tomorrow."

14

Wilson's plan was supposed to swing into action the next morning. But first there was the matter of the Five Dwarfs and the bus stop tax.

"Know what, guys?" Dusty said to Wilson and me at the bus stop. "I'm starting to wonder if Amazing Nature Girl is right. Maybe we shouldn't take any more candy from the single digits."

"But they bring extra for us," Wilson argued.

"I know, but it's mostly stuff we don't like anyway," said Dusty. "And I don't like the idea that people think we're picking on little kids."

"I have to agree with Dusty," I said.

"Two against one," Dusty said to Wilson, then turned to the dwarf pod. "Guess what, guys? As of today we're officially suspending the bus stop tax. You don't have to give us any more candy."

You would have thought the Five Dwarfs

would be happy, but they mostly frowned and looked puzzled. Then the bus came, and my friends and I got on. All the way to school Wilson talked about his plan to demolish the Psycho Lunch Monitors from H.E.L.L.

"They'll never know what hit them," he said with a happy glint in his eyes as our bus pulled into school.

"Ahem!" Dusty cleared his throat and nodded out the window. "I hate to say this, dudes, but they may already know."

Wilson and I looked out the window. Monkey Breath was standing in the bus circle, pointing a finger at us. Grandma opened the bus door. The single digits got out, then Amazing Nature Girl and Melody. As my friends and I followed, we glanced out the window. Our principal was frowning, and the lines between his eyes formed a deep V.

"He looks really mad angry," Wilson muttered nervously.

"He *always* looks mad angry," said Dusty.

My friends and I got off the bus. Monkey Breath glared at Wilson. "Would you like to explain why you gave some first and second graders a dangerous weapon?"

"What are you talking about?" Wilson asked.

"A four-edged knife that looks like it could cut a square right through you," said Monkey Breath.

"A four-edged knife?" Wilson repeated with a frown.

"The Decrustifyer," I said.

"It's for cutting the crusts off sandwiches," Wilson explained.

Monkey Breath narrowed his eyes suspiciously.

"Come on, Principal Chump," Dusty said. "Do you really think we'd give little kids a dangerous weapon?"

"Well . . . maybe not, but you do try to break every rule in the book," our principal said.

"Actually, that's not true," I pointed out. "We never break an existing rule. If we did, you'd punish us, right?"

"If I could catch you," said Monkey Breath.

"You catch us all the time," Dusty said.

"But it's always for things that aren't in the rule books," Monkey Breath said.

"Exactly my point!" I said. "Don't you see that we're helping you?"

"How?" asked Monkey Breath.

"We're exploring the unknown," I said.

"We go where no rule has gone before," added Dusty.

"How many new rules have we helped you create this year alone?" I asked.

Monkey Breath scratched his head. "I don't know. A couple of dozen, at least."

"See?" Dusty said. "If it wasn't for us, kids

might be breaking those rules for years to come, and you'd never know."

"I guess." Monkey Breath rubbed his chin thoughtfully.

"I think you owe us a big thanks," I said.

Monkey Breath squinted at me. "Don't push your luck, Kyle. The three of you, get out of here. And no more Decrustifyers."

"Aren't you going to make it a rule?" I asked.

Monkey Breath's eyes widened. "Why, of course! Cafeteria rule number six hundred eighty-five, *The possession of Decrustifyers on school property is strictly forbidden.* I must go tell Ms. Fortune right away!"

Our principal hurried back toward school.

"That guy is twisted," Wilson muttered.

Dusty agreed. "*Seriously* twisted."

My friends and I went through the upper-grade school entrance. Hard Marks has two entrances. One for the kids in kindergarten through fifth grade and one for the upper school, sixth through eighth grades.

Inside, Wilson stopped and turned to us. "Okay, guys, you've got your materials?"

"Check," said Dusty.

"You'll have to work fast," Wilson warned.

"We know," I said.

"You'll need that can-do attitude," said Wilson.

"Got it," said Dusty.

We clasped hands and repeated our new slogan. "We go where no rule has gone before."

"Catch you at lunch," said Wilson.

He headed for the TV station. Dusty and I headed for the cafeteria. The war was about to begin.

Sabotage is a fine art. And the best sabotage isn't obvious at first. At lunchtime, we stood near the doorway to the cafeteria and watched as the first kids came out of the lunch line and headed for their assigned tables.

But no one found their assigned table. Instead they began to wander around with puzzled looks on their faces. Pretty soon there was a big crowd of kids milling around like a bunch of ants whose tunnel has been blocked.

"Sit down!" Big Bertha ordered. "Find your assigned seat and sit!"

"But we can't find our assigned seats," someone answered.

Wanda the Widebody and Big Bertha started looking at the walls. Table one was now Table seventy-one. Table six was now fifty-six. Table twelve was now two hundred twelve. Meanwhile, kids kept coming into the cafeteria with lunch boxes and bags, and more kids were coming out of the lunch line with trays. The confused, milling crowd was growing larger.

Wanda the Widebody grabbed her radio. "Lunchroom to office! Code red! We need Principal Chump STAT!"

By the time Monkey Breath and Ms. Fortune arrived, the cafeteria was a madhouse. Kids were all over the place. A lot wanted to sit down, but every time they tried, the Psycho Lunch Moni-

53

tors from H.E.L.L. would make them get up because they weren't in their correct seats.

"What's going on here?" Monkey Breath asked.

Wanda the Widebody and Big Bertha pointed at the new table numbers on the walls. Monkey Breath's jaw dropped. "Someone changed them!"

It's interesting how kids always assume that grown-ups know what to do. Especially grown-ups like principals and lunch monitors who are supposed to be specially trained. From the looks on Monkey Breath's face and the faces of the Psycho Lunch Monitors from H.E.L.L., it was pretty obvious that they didn't have a clue.

Finally, Ms. Fortune leaned over to Monkey Breath (she's a lot taller than he is, especially in those red high heels) and whispered something in his ear. Monkey Breath nodded.

"All right, everyone, quiet down," he announced to the crowd.

"QUIET!" Big Bertha bellowed.

Meanwhile, Monkey Breath straightened his tie. He always did that before making a major announcement.

"Okay, here's what we're going to do," he told the crowd. "Since the table numbers have apparently been vandalized, and you don't know which table is yours, for today only you may sit wherever you like."

54

All over the cafeteria, kids surged toward the tables. My friends and I took our time and sat down at the table we always sat at before the Psycho Lunch Monitors from H.E.L.L. arrived.

"You have to be impressed with their ability to think on their feet," Wilson said with a smile.

"I know what you mean," I agreed. "Who would have thought of letting us sit wherever we wanted?"

"No talking!"

My friends and I looked up, startled to find Wanda the Widebody glaring at us.

"Just because you can sit wherever you want doesn't mean you can talk, too," she snapped.

Now Monkey Breath joined her. "Boys, I'd like to see your hands."

Dusty frowned, then pulled out a deck of cards and began to deal them.

"What are you doing?" Monkey Breath asked.

"You said you wanted to see our hands," Dusty said. "So I'm dealing the cards so we can show you."

"Not *card* hands," Monkey Breath sputtered. "Your *real* hands. The ones attached to your arms."

My friends and I held up our hands. Monkey Breath inspected them closely, then turned to Wanda the Widebody. "No trace of paint."

Wanda and our principal moved to other tables. As soon as they were gone, Wilson reached into his pocket and pulled out a thin latex glove like the kind the lunch ladies wore. The glove was streaked with paint.

"Good thing Monkey Breath didn't ask to see our gloves," he said with a wink.

After school my friends and I got together in the TV station to review the day's tape from the remote camera over Mr. Recycling Box.

"I have to hand it to you, Wilson," Dusty said. "This is one of the most brilliant plans I've ever seen. A two-pronged attack. Not only do we drive the Psycho Lunch Monitors crazy by messing up everything they're trying to do, but we collect embarrassing video of them to show to the whole school."

Wilson beamed proudly. "I've even graphed it. Check it out."

He pulled a folded piece of paper out of his pocket and smoothed it out on the desk.

"Let's see the videotape," I said.

"Right." Wilson punched some buttons, and a grainy gray picture of the empty cafeteria appeared on one of the TV screens in front of us. He pushed another button and the tape began to race. In hyperspeed, the breakfast-program kids

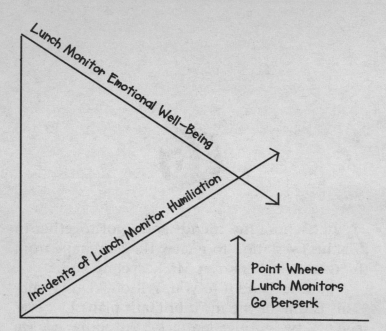

Lunch Monitor Emotional Well-Being

Incidents of Lunch Monitor Humiliation

Point Where
Lunch Monitors
Go Berserk

arrived, dumped their backpacks, and scurried into and out of the kitchen with their breakfasts. It was funny to watch them wolf down their food in a matter of seconds, then grab their backpacks and scurry off again.

Next, Sam the custodian raced through the cafeteria pushing a broom so fast she looked like a little machine. A couple of lunch ladies came out of the kitchen and started speed-wiping the breakfast tables.

Next came a minute or two of tape showing the empty cafeteria again. Then Sam pulled out the gray garbage cans for lunch, and the lunch ladies set up the cookie and ice cream stands.

Then the Psycho Lunch Monitors from H.E.L.L. arrived.

"Slow it down," Dusty said.

"Let's hope they do something really embarrassing," I said.

Wilson slowed the tape, and we watched Wanda the Widebody and Big Bertha stand in the empty lunchroom. They spoke to each other in serious, muted voices, as if they were afraid "the enemy" might overhear them.

Then kids began to come into the cafeteria for lunch, and Bertha and Wanda started to yell at them to get in line and not talk.

"Hey, look." I pointed at the upper left-hand corner of the screen. "There's us."

My friends and I were just visible on the grainy black-and-white screen, standing in the doorway.

"Here's where it gets good," Wilson said. On the screen, kids began to come out of the lunch line and look for their tables. Since we'd changed all the table numbers, the crowd began to mill around and grow, and the lunch monitors began to freak.

"We already saw this," I said. "Do we have to watch it again?"

"Kyle's right," said Dusty. "Let's skip it."

Wilson fast-forwarded the tape through the scenes of Monkey Breath arriving and Ms. Fortune suggesting he let kids sit where they liked. After that, it was a normal lunch until the cafeteria emptied out and Sam came back to start cleaning up.

"Hold it," Dusty said.

Wilson slowed down the tape just as Wanda the Widebody and Big Bertha came out of the kitchen carrying trays of their own and sat down at a table with their backs to the camera.

"Interesting." Dusty rubbed his chin.

"That they eat a school lunch after everyone leaves?" Wilson asked.

"Who would have thought?" Dusty muttered to himself.

"Who would have *cared*?" Wilson started to fast-forward the tape again.

"Wait." Dusty stopped him. "Go back."

"Why?" asked Wilson.

"Just do it."

Wilson rewound the tape. Once again we watched the lunch monitors sit down to eat.

"There!" Dusty suddenly said.

"What?" Wilson stopped the tape.

"Run it again slowly," said Dusty.

"This is stupid," Wilson complained, but he reran the tape anyway. Dusty leaned close to the monitor screen.

"Darn," he muttered.

"What is it?" I asked.

"Nothing." Dusty shrugged. "Probably just my imagination."

"I could have told you that." Wilson let the tape fast-forward. We watched briefly as Sam

60

raced through the cafeteria sweeping and mopping while the lunch ladies speed-wiped the tables. Next, kids zipped through on their way to catch their buses.

And then the tape was over.

"Well, that was a big fat nothing," Dusty mumbled.

"Maybe not," I said.

"The Psycho Lunch Monitors didn't do anything embarrassing," Wilson said.

"Not the lunch monitors. Someone else," I said. "Wilson, go back to lunchtime and roll the tape."

Wilson rewound the tape to lunch and started playing it again. "Now what are we looking for?"

"That." I pointed at the screen as Alice Appleford came out of the lunch line carrying a tray with a bunch of clear plastic containers with salad in them.

"So?" asked Wilson. "She's eating salads."

"*Five* of them?" I asked.

"Guess she was feeling *extra* healthy today," Dusty cracked.

But as we watched, Alice sat down and mostly talked to her friends while she slowly picked through one salad. You could see that she wasn't enjoying it. She'd spear something with her fork and then frown at it for a moment before putting it in her mouth. Then she'd make an unhappy face while she slowly chewed and swallowed.

"Why'd she get so many salads if she doesn't like them?" Dusty wondered out loud.

"Watch," I said.

After a while, Alice picked up her tray and headed over to the garbage and recycling area. She'd eaten half of one salad. She stopped beside the big gray garbage can and quickly glanced around to make sure no one was watching her. Then she dumped all the salads into the garbage can and tossed the empty containers into Mr. Recycling Box.

"I can't believe she chucked all that salad," Wilson said.

"Makes perfect sense to me," I said. "Right, Dusty?"

"That is pathetic," Dusty grumbled. "She didn't want the salad. She just wanted the containers so she can win the recycling contest."

"You got it," I said. "That proves she doesn't care about raising anyone's consciousness. All she cares about is winning. If there was a major polluting contest next week, I promise you she'd be collecting chemicals to dump in the river."

"Not like anyone would be surprised," Wilson said.

"Can you save it?" I asked.

"The Alice segment?" Wilson said. "Sure. But why?"

"Could make great blackmail material someday," I said with a smile.

The next day at lunch my friends and I again paused in the doorway to the cafeteria and watched. Overnight, Monkey Breath had put up new table numbers on the walls. Each number was protected by Plexiglas so no one could change it.

So this time when the kids came out of the lunch line, it was easy for them to see which table was theirs. Finding their assigned seats was another story. Pretty soon it looked the same as it had the day before — a big crowd of kids milling around with confused looks on their faces.

"Sit down!" Big Bertha ordered.

"Sit in your assigned seats!" commanded Wanda the Widebody.

"But we don't know which seat to sit in," a kid complained.

"Go to your table and find your letter," said Big Bertha.

"Which letter?" asked another kid. "There are zillions of them."

Deep wrinkles appeared in Wanda the Widebody's broad forehead. She and Big Bertha went to investigate. In no time they were on the radio with Principal Chump. A moment later Monkey Breath and Ms. Fortune rushed into the lunchroom and told everyone to sit wherever they liked. My friends and I sat down at our favorite table.

"Make room, dudes." Cheech the Leech put his tray down. "Fess up, guys. Everyone knows you're the ones who changed the table numbers and seat letters."

"Don't know what you're talking about," I said.

Meanwhile, Monkey Breath was making a huge group of single digits get up and march through the cafeteria. Farty and Burpy were in the front of the line. Their eyes were red, and tears were running down their cheeks.

"What's going on?" I asked as they passed our table.

"Principal Chump's making us go to the office because we have paint on our hands," Farty answered with a sob.

"We didn't do anything," Burpy wailed.

I turned to my friends and whispered, "They're rounding up the single digits!"

Wilson's jaw dropped. "Monkey Breath thinks they did it!"

"But little kids *always* have paint on their hands," said Dusty.

"That's great!" said Cheech. "They'll take the blame instead of you guys."

My friends and I shared a worried look. Cheech couldn't have been more wrong. We didn't want the single digits to get blamed. Ms. Fortune was coming from the other side of the cafeteria and I got up to speak to her.

"Sit down!" Big Bertha shouted, but I ignored her.

"What's the problem, Kyle?" Ms. Fortune asked.

I quickly explained why Monkey Breath was rounding up the single digits.

"Oh, no!" Ms. Fortune groaned and hurried toward our principal. We watched as she stopped him and started to explain why he couldn't send a hundred little kids to the office.

"But they're the only ones with paint on their hands," Monkey Breath argued.

I raised my hand. "Excuse me, Principal Chump."

"What, Kyle?" Monkey Breath asked impatiently.

"Maybe the painter wore gloves," I said.

Monkey Breath frowned. "What kind of gloves?"

"Like these." Dusty pointed at a pair of paint-smeared latex gloves lying on the floor behind Cheech.

Monkey Breath picked them up. "Where did these come from?"

"They must have fallen out of Cheech's pocket," said Wilson.

Monkey Breath's forehead wrinkled. He pointed a finger at Cheech. "You, to the office immediately!"

"But I didn't do it!" Cheech screeched.

"We'll see about that," Monkey Breath growled.

Cheech got up slowly. "I'll get you guys for this," he threatened as he left.

That afternoon when school ended, my friends and I once again gathered in the TV station.

"Any news on Cheech?" I asked.

"I heard he got off," Dusty said. "Monkey Breath couldn't prove the gloves were his."

"Because they *weren't* his," said Wilson as he started to fast-forward that day's tape. We all stared at the black-and-white monitor.

"The same old boring stuff," Wilson mumbled.

"Maybe not," Dusty said as we watched the end of lunch. "It's Gary and Melody."

"So?" Wilson slowed the tape. On the screen, Gary and Melody were standing at Mr. Recycling Box, talking.

"Look at that smile on her face," Dusty said. "She's up to something."

Wilson pushed a lever and the sound grew louder.

"So what could we do to make Hart TV better?" Melody asked on the tape.

"Are you serious?" Gary replied. "Get rid of Alice. She's the most boring person in the world. And forget all those stupid stories about school projects. No one cares about that junk."

Wilson froze the tape and turned to us with a big grin. "I bet Alice would just *love* to see this."

Dusty and I were grinning, too. "Keep going," I said. "This is great." Wilson started the tape again.

"But isn't that what Principal Chump wants the TV station to do?" asked Melody.

"Principal Chump is the biggest idiot on the face of the earth," Gary replied with a snort. "He's so stupid I'm surprised his knuckles don't drag on the ground when he walks. TV in this school should be the same as everywhere else. It's about entertainment."

"What would you do?" Melody asked.

"We could have a game show," Gary said. "Or a talk thing like the *Late Show*."

"With you as the host?" Melody asked.

"You think anyone else in this school could do it?" Gary puffed out his chest.

Wilson froze the tape and turned to us with the biggest grin I'd ever seen. "Gary Gordon is dead meat!"

"Definitely," I said. "But don't forget our mission isn't to nail Gary, it's to eliminate the Psycho Lunch Ladies from H.E.L.L."

"He's right," said Dusty. "We still don't have anything good on Bertha and Wanda."

"Let's keep watching," I said.

Wilson started the tape again. After Gary and Melody, it was pretty much the same as the day before. Lunch ended and the two lunch monitors came out of the kitchen with trays, then sat down with their backs to the camera and started to eat.

"Nothing useful," Wilson grumbled.

"Wait," said Dusty. "Go back to them coming out of the kitchen."

Wilson rolled the tape back and started it again.

"Can you run it slower?" Dusty asked.

Wilson ran the tape slower. We watched Big Bertha and Wanda carrying their trays.

"See how many desserts each of them has?" Dusty asked.

Wilson and I squinted at the monitor. Even though the picture was black-and-white, it was easy to see the cups of chocolate pudding and whipped cream because of the contrast between the dark pudding and the light whipped cream.

"Looks like they each have two," I said.

"Right," said Dusty. "Now keep watching."

We watched the lunch monitors sit down with their backs to the camera and start to eat.

"There! There!" Dusty said excitedly. "Freeze it, Wilson!"

Wilson stopped the tape. We all squinted at the screen.

"I see it!" I gasped. You could just barely tell that Big Bertha had scooped up a spoonful of chocolate pudding and whipped cream.

"You see it, Wilson?" Dusty asked.

"Hardly," said Wilson. "You think she's eating her dessert first?"

"Definitely." I gave Dusty a high five. "We did it, dude! We nailed them. Just wait until the whole school sees this!"

"Forget it," said Wilson.

Dusty and I stopped celebrating. "Why?"

"You think kids sitting in classrooms are going to be able to see that?" Wilson asked. "No way. I'm sitting here a foot from the screen and I can barely see it."

"Can't you blow it up or something?" I asked.

"Sorry, dude." Wilson shook his head. "That takes seriously advanced technology."

"Then what do we do?" asked Dusty.

"We get it on tape," I said.

"But it's too late," Wilson said. "It happened hours ago."

"I know," I said with a smile. "But if it happened once . . . it'll happen again."

The Challenge: To tape the Psycho Lunch Monitors from H.E.L.L. eating dessert first.

The Problem: The camera over Mr. Recycling Box isn't close enough.

The Solution: ????????????

Wilson tugged at his earlobe, then blinked as if a lightbulb had gone on in his head. "I've got it! We'll dress up like lunch ladies!"

"We?" I repeated with a firm shake of my head. "Sorry, dude, there's no way."

"Okay, okay," Wilson said. *"I'll* dress up like a lunch lady."

"And what?" Dusty asked. "Go up to the Psycho Lunch Monitors and ask them politely to turn around and face the camera while they eat dessert first?"

Wilson smiled back devilishly. "No. Because we'll have a secret weapon." He paused dramatically. "Gentlemen, it's time to introduce the Lunch Lady Cam."

Only Wilson could have come up with the Lunch Lady Cam. "It's a tiny camera, held in place on your head by a hairnet," he explained later as he, Dusty, and I skateboarded over to Melody's house. Melody had volunteered to help Wilson dress up like a lunch lady.

"Held in place on *your* head," I reminded him.

Melody lives in a one-story house near the highway. She met us at the door with a smile. "Hi, Wilson, ready to be a lunch lady?"

Wilson grinned. "Definitely!"

"Then follow me." Melody led us into her room. It was a total girl's room. You'd know it even if you'd been led in blindfolded. First of all, it smelled like a girl's room. Sort of a mixture of perfume and fresh laundry.

Second, the walls were pink (a dead giveaway).

Third, the bed was made. Lined up in front of a lacy pillow were three stuffed brown dogs. Laid out on the bed was a dress that looked exactly like the ones the lunch ladies wore. It was light blue with buttons in front and short sleeves.

Melody handed it to Wilson. "Here you go."

Wilson took the dress and stared at it. He seemed to freeze.

"You can put it on in the bathroom." Melody pointed through the doorway.

"Uh, er, okay." Wilson didn't move.

"What's the problem?" I asked.

"Well, uh, I'm not sure how," Wilson stammered.

"How what?" Dusty asked.

"How you put it on," said Wilson.

Melody laughed. "You have a choice. You can either unbutton the buttons and put it on like a shirt, or you can just slide it over your head, bottom first."

Wilson turned the garment around as if he was trying to find the bottom. Melody gently aimed him out of the room, down the hall, and toward the bathroom. Then she turned back to Dusty and me. "He must *really* want to get rid of those lunch monitors."

A few moments later, Wilson came back into the room wearing the dress. The bottom dragged on the floor and the shoulders hung halfway down his arms.

"What do you think, guys?" he asked.

Melody shook her head. "Sorry, it's too big for you."

"Do you have a smaller one," Wilson asked.

"I'm afraid not," Melody answered.

"Maybe you can change this one," Dusty said. "Like sew it smaller."

Melody shook her head. "My mom needs it. She still works as a lunch lady sometimes."

"Then maybe we can pad it," Wilson said hopefully. "Like with pillows."

"Gee, Wilson, I never knew you wanted to wear a dress so badly," Dusty joked.

"I don't!" Wilson sputtered. "All I want is the right to eat dessert first."

"I hate to say this, but I really can't think of a way to make that dress fit you, Wilson," Melody said.

Wilson's shoulders sagged with disappointment.

"Guess you'll just have to come up with another plan," Dusty said.

Wilson gazed at the floor. Then he raised his head and his whole face seemed to brighten. "Not another plan, Dusty, another *man*!"

Wilson pointed his finger at Dusty. "You're the man, dude. Maybe I can't wear this dress, but you can!"

"Me?" Dusty looked surprised.

"Sure, come on," Wilson said. "I would have done it if the dress fit."

"If the dress fits, wear it." I chuckled.

"Sure, but — "

"No buts." Wilson stuffed the dress into Dusty's hands and pushed him toward the door. "You can wear it, Dusty. Just think of the service you'll be doing for your school."

"What service?" Dusty dug his feet into the carpet.

"Getting rid of the Psycho Lunch Monitors from H.E.L.L. and defeating the evil empire of Dr. Monkey Breath," Wilson said, still pushing him.

"I don't have to wear a dress to defeat Monkey

Breath," Dusty argued. "All I need is a couple of hundred frogs and some smoke bombs."

"Yeah, right." Wilson pushed him out of Melody's bedroom. "And you can get suspended for the rest of your life."

Dusty went down the hall to the bathroom. A little while later he came back wearing the dress. The bottom wasn't dragging on the floor anymore, but as with Wilson, the shoulders hung halfway down his arms.

Melody shook her head sadly. "Sorry, Dusty, it doesn't fit you, either."

I can't say that Dusty looked real unhappy. In a flash he spun around and headed back to the bathroom to change.

Wilson pursed his lips and looked really frustrated. "There has to be a way, there just *has* to be. We have to find someone who's tall enough and who has broad shoulders."

He looked me. A smile appeared on his face. "Like *you*, Kyle."

"**W**ait a minute!" I gasped.

"Don't you think he's tall enough and has broad enough shoulders?" Wilson asked Melody.

"I think you're right," Melody answered.

"Whoa! No way!" I started to back away. "Sorry. You've got the wrong guy. I mean, the *way* wrong guy. Because there is no way. Absolutely, positively no way!"

"No way what?" asked Dusty, who now appeared in the doorway with the dress in his arms.

"No way I am putting on that thing," I said. "No way I am wearing a wig and a hairnet."

"Why not?" Dusty asked with a grin. "I think you'd look kind of cute."

I made a fist. "You want to see cute?"

"Now, now," Wilson said. "There's no reason to feel threatened, Kyle. Dusty and I were willing to wear the dress. But it didn't fit us. You, on the other hand, would probably fit into it perfectly."

"Too bad you'll never know," I shot back.

"Hey, weren't you the guy who said, 'If the dress fits, wear it'?" Dusty asked with a smile.

"Naw, that was someone else," I said.

"You don't want to defeat the evil empire of Dr. Monkey Breath?" Wilson asked.

"You want to go through the rest of your life eating lunch in assigned seats and not being able to talk?" asked Dusty.

"It's not the rest of my life," I said. "It's the rest of the school year."

"But think of the favor you'll be doing for all the kids who follow." Dusty put the dress in my hands. "Think of the Five Dwarfs. Here you go, dude."

The light blue material felt weird. It was sort of thin and slippery and not like anything my clothes were made of.

"You can do it, Kyle," Dusty said.

"I know I can," I answered. "The question is, do I *want* to?"

"Think of life without Big Bertha and Wanda the Widebody," said Wilson. "Think of being able to eat dessert any old time you want. These are causes men wear dresses for, Kyle."

"What are you talking about?" I asked.

Wilson shrugged. "I don't know. Just put on the stupid dress, okay?"

I let out a big sigh and started toward the bathroom. "I don't believe I'm doing this. I really, really don't."

I can't say that the dress fit, but I will admit that I seemed to fill it better than Wilson or Dusty. Melody got some safety pins and pinned the back to make it fit even better.

"What about the wig and hairnet?" she asked.

"I'll bring that stuff tomorrow," said Dusty.

Wilson insisted on taking the dress home. He was certain I'd "forget" to bring it to school the next day. The next morning I was eating breakfast with my little brother, Scott, and my mom when the phone rang. Mom answered it and held the receiver toward me. "It's for you."

I took the phone.

"Hey, Kyle, you coming to school?" It was Wilson.

"What do you think?" I said.

"I think you're seriously thinking about skipping today," Wilson said. "Don't do it, dude."

"Yeah, yeah, I hear ya." I hung up. Truth is, the idea of skipping school that day had crossed my mind. But if I got nailed with an unexplained absence, my mom would shoot me.

A little later I met Dusty and Wilson at the bus stop. Wilson had a big smile on his face. He turned to Dusty and held out his palm. "Hand it over, dude."

Dusty reached into his pocket and pulled out a Game Boy cartridge. Wilson took it.

"What's that about?" I asked.

"A side bet." Wilson pocketed the cartridge. "Dusty was sure you were going to skip. I bet him you'd show."

"That's why you called to make sure," I said.

"Hey, this means a lot to me," said Wilson.

"You have the dress and the Lunch Lady Cam?" Dusty asked him.

Wilson patted his backpack. "Right here. You have the wig and the hairnet?"

"In the bag," answered Dusty.

The bus pulled up. The Five Dwarfs and Amazing Nature Girl got on. Then my friends and I. Grandma gave us a big smile. "Good morning, boys."

We said hello and went to our regular seats in the back. I slumped down and stared out the window. A little while later, the bus stopped and Melody got on. When she saw me, her eyes widened.

"Wow, I really didn't think I'd see you here this morning," she said.

"So I've been told," I replied.

Melody reached over the seat and put her hand on my arm. "Don't worry, handsome, I won't think any less of you for wearing a dress."

Dusty reached over and put his hand on my arm. He batted his eyes and said, "And neither will I, honey bunch."

Dusty and Wilson were waiting in the hall for me before lunch.

"Time to go," Wilson said.

"What's the rush?" I asked. "The lunch monitors don't eat until after lunchtime."

"We have to prepare you," said Dusty.

We headed down to the cafeteria. Kids were quietly coming out of the lunch line and finding their assigned seats. During the night, Monkey Breath had all the seat lettering redone. Under the watchful eyes of the Psycho Lunch Monitors from H.E.L.L., kids all over the cafeteria were eating silently.

"Over here," Wilson whispered. At one end of the lunch room was a small stage with curtains. My friends had decided it was the best place for me to change.

Melody was waiting on the stage for us. Her eyes were sparkling, and she had a big grin on her face.

"I wish you wouldn't look at me like that," I said.

"It's okay, Kyle," she said. "Just remember. I'm laughing *with* you, not *at* you."

"Yeah, well, I don't know how you can be laughing *with* me if I'm not laughing," I muttered.

Wilson opened his backpack and took out the dress.

"I can't believe I let you guys talk me into this." I groaned as my friends helped me put it on.

"Where's the wig and hairnet?" asked Melody.

"Right here." Dusty opened his backpack and took out a red-white-and-blue-striped wig. It was about the size of a basketball and shaped like an Afro.

Wilson, Melody, and I stared at it in disbelief.

"This is a joke, right?" asked Wilson.

Dusty shook his head. "No, why?"

"Dusty, have you ever seen a lunch lady with a red-white-and-blue Afro?" Melody asked.

Dusty rubbed his jaw. "Well, now that you mention it . . . I guess not."

"This is ridiculous." I started to pull off the dress. "There's no way I can go out there in that wig. They'll notice right away."

"Wait!" Wilson turned to Melody. "Once it's under the hairnet it won't be that obvious, will it?"

"Well . . ." Melody seemed unsure.

Wilson turned back to me. "Come on, Kyle. All we need is a glimpse of them. It's not like you have to stand there staring."

I gave Dusty a questioning look.

"You want my honest opinion?" he asked.

"Yes."

"When the going gets tough," he said, holding up the wig, "the tough guys wear wigs."

"**O**kay, here's the hard part." Wilson bent down and lifted a small black case out of his pack. "We have to be really careful with this."

He took out a tiny camera with a thin black wire hanging down from the back. "This thing costs a mint, so we can't mess it up. Stand really still, Kyle."

He gently placed the camera in the wig on my head. "Now, don't move." Next I felt something go into my ear.

"What's that?" I asked.

"Earpiece," Wilson said. "So I can direct you from the control room. Melody, got the hairnet?"

"Right here." Melody stood up on a chair and carefully placed the hairnet over the wig and my head. Next, Wilson and Dusty ran the wire under the collar of the dress and down behind my back. Now that the camera and wig were all in place, Melody gently tucked the wig hair under the hairnet.

"You know, Wilson was right," she said. "With the hairnet on the wig, it isn't so obvious that it's red, white, and blue."

"Not unless you look at it," Dusty cracked.

I felt my jaw drop.

"Hey, just kidding." Dusty had a goofy grin on his face. "Oh, man, this is better than I ever imagined."

"This is nothing." Wilson chuckled. "Wait until Melody puts the makeup on him!"

You can guess how I reacted when Wilson said I would have to wear makeup or I wouldn't look enough like a lunch lady.

"What are you talking about?" I sputtered. "I have red-white-and-blue hair! I already don't look like a lunch lady. I look like a clown!"

I was just about to yank off the wig when Wilson screamed that if I made any fast moves the camera would go totally out of whack. Finally, I agreed to let Melody put a little bit of makeup on my lips, cheeks, and eyes. Dusty and Wilson were both grinning like fools.

"What a babe!" Dusty said gleefully.

"What's your name, sweetie?" Wilson asked.

"Kyle."

"That's not a girl's name," said Dusty.

"I think it'll have to be Kylee," said Melody.

Out in the cafeteria, the Psycho Lunch Monitors from H.E.L.L. were starting to call tables to return their trays and throw away their garbage.

"I'd better get some lunch before the period ends." Melody left to eat.

Dusty and Wilson stayed with me behind the curtain.

"You have to get as close to the lunch monitors as possible while they're eating," said Wilson. "Wipe the tables right near them. The thing is, if you look up they'll see your face, and they're gonna know right away something's wrong. So you have to keep your head down."

"If my head's down, won't the camera be taking pictures of the floor?" I asked.

"No, I've got it aimed so that when your head is down, it's looking right at the lunch monitors," Wilson explained. "Don't forget I'll be speaking to you through the earpiece and telling you how to move your head."

Finally, Wilson pulled a large Ziploc bag out of his backpack and took something cold and damp out of it and handed it to me. "Your rag, Miss Kylee."

Briinnngg! The bell rang and lunch ended. Wilson had gone to the TV station to direct me, and Dusty went with him to watch. I waited behind the curtain with the damp rag in my hand and listened to the shuffling of footsteps and murmurs of kids trying to talk but not be heard.

"No talking!" ordered Big Bertha.

"Leave in single file!" commanded Wanda the Widebody.

"Kyle?" The voice in the earpiece caught me by surprise. It was Wilson, speaking from the TV station.

"Yes?" I answered.

"Don't bother answering," Wilson said through the earpiece. *"You don't have a mike. Just listen. Bend your head down until I say stop."*

I started to bend my head down until I was looking at my feet.

"There! That's perfect!" said Wilson. *"That's the position you need to be in for me to get a good picture*

of the lunch monitors. Now, stick your head around the curtain and see what they're doing."

With my head down, I tried to part the curtain.

"No, dummy!" Wilson screeched. *"Use your eyes. You don't have to have your head down now. You just have to do it later when you're near them."*

I raised my head and peeked out through the curtains. The kids had left the cafeteria, and the Psycho Lunch Monitors from H.E.L.L. were just coming out of the kitchen with their lunches. Like the days before, they were both carrying trays with at least two desserts on them.

I climbed down off the stage and walked through the lunchroom. As soon as I was in their line of vision, I put my head down and started wiping the tabletops.

"Okay, good," Wilson said through the earpiece. *"Move your head a little to the right. Now down a little more. Good, good! Now just a hair to the left. Perfect!"*

All I could see was the table I was wiping, but I assumed that through the Lunch Lady Cam, Wilson could see the Psycho Lunch Monitors from H.E.L.L. eating their lunches.

"Move two tables closer," Wilson said through the earpiece.

I felt a shiver and swallowed hard. My heart started beating faster. Two tables closer meant I'd be only one table away from the Psycho Lunch

Monitors. If one of them looked up and spotted me, I was dead meat.

"Come on, get closer!" Wilson urged through the earpiece. *"They're gonna start eating any second!"*

I took a deep breath and went to the next table, wiping spots here and there so it wouldn't look too obvious. Next, I reached the target table.

"Great!" Wilson said through the earpiece. *"Put your head down a little more and slightly to the right. Perfect!"*

I was so close I could hear the lunch monitors talking.

"Finally, a normal day," Big Bertha said.

"Yeah," agreed Wanda the Widebody. "Those brats are starting to learn."

They stopped speaking. I assumed they were eating.

"Whatever you do, don't look up," Wilson said gleefully through the earpiece. *"They're doing it. Both of them! They're eating dessert first! This is perfect! Just wait until . . . Oh, no!"*

I felt another shiver but fought the temptation to look up. Something was wrong. I kept wiping the table, waiting to hear what Wilson would say next.

When Wilson's voice came back through the earpiece, it was dead serious. *"Quick, turn around to the table behind you and start wiping. Get away from the lunch monitors as fast as you can. And keep your head down!"*

I did what I was told, but I couldn't figure out what had gone wrong until I heard a voice say, "Hello, ladies, so how did it go today?"

It was Monkey Breath!

26

Keeping my head down, I kept wiping and moving away from the table where the Psycho Lunch Monitors from H.E.L.L. were chatting with our school principal.

"Keep going toward the exit," Wilson said through the earpiece. *"Dusty's on his way to help you get out of the dress."*

I kept wiping and walking toward the exit.

"Uh, excuse me!" Monkey Breath called out behind me.

My heart started to beat harder, and it was suddenly difficult to breathe. My knees felt rubbery.

"Uh, you, lunch lady!" Monkey Breath called. "I'm afraid you've missed some tables."

"Go, Kyle!" Wilson yelled in my ear.

I went on autopilot, pretending not to hear Monkey Breath, and just hurrying toward the exit.

"Hey, wait!" Monkey Breath yelled behind me.

I was running now. All I could think about was getting out of there. And getting out of those clothes. I got to the lunchroom doors, yanked one open, and —

Slap! A hand landed hard on my shoulder. I was spun around and came face-to-face with Monkey Breath.

His eyes went wide. "What the — ?"

"Uh-oh!" Wilson gasped through the earpiece.

I heard rapid footsteps. A split second later Dusty came running around the corner and skidded to a stop.

Monkey Breath stared at him and then back at me. His eyes went to the wig and hairnet. He frowned, then yanked something out of the wig. It was the Lunch Lady Cam.

"What in the world?" he said.

"Hey! Everything went blank!" Wilson said through the earpiece. He must have said it too loud, because Monkey Breath's eyes instantly fixed on my ear.

The last words I heard Wilson say were *"What's he doing?"* Then Monkey Breath yanked the earpiece out of my ear.

He clenched his teeth in fury. "Go directly to the office and wait for me." He turned to Dusty. "And you go with him."

Our principal stomped away down the hall.

"Where's he going?" Dusty asked.

"To nail Wilson, where else?" I hung my head. "Come on, we might as well go down to the office."

"**W**hat kills me is how Monkey Breath instantly decides that you guys are also involved," I said as we headed for the office. "I mean, sure, it's obvious I'm involved because I'm standing there wearing a dress and a wig. But how come he sent you down here, too?"

"I guess I fit the criminal profile," Dusty said with a shrug.

Ms. Fortune was in the office when we arrived. She gave me a funny look. "Did I miss something? It's not Dress-Like-a-Lunch-Lady Day, is it?"

"No, Ms. Fortune," I said.

"Why do I have a feeling I'm going to be writing up a new rule?" she said with a sigh.

The office door swung open, and Monkey Breath stomped in with Wilson. Our principal's face was red, and he looked as angry as a five-and-a-half-foot-tall man with big ears can look.

"Wait here," he growled, then stormed into his room, slamming the door behind him.

"Uh-oh," Ms. Fortune mumbled. "We may be looking at *multiple* new rules today."

Dusty sat back on the bench, put his hands behind his head, and stretched out. Wilson sat hunched over, chewing on a fingernail and tapping his foot nervously. As for me, I guess I just assumed that I was in major trouble.

The minutes passed slowly. Today it seemed like Monkey Breath was making us wait longer than usual. Finally, Dusty caught Ms. Fortune's eye. "Why's he making us wait so long?"

Ms. Fortune looked down at her phone. "He's been on the phone. Oops. He just got off."

The door opened, and Monkey Breath beckoned us in. "Take your regular seats, boys."

My friends and I went in and sat down. The curtains were closed, and the office was dim. I glanced again at the weird soundproofing on the walls and wondered if kids really were tortured in there. Monkey Breath went behind his desk and pulled out the thick blue binder entitled *School and Cafeteria Rules*.

"Well, boys, I suppose congratulations are due," he said as he thumbed through the binder. "Just when I thought you couldn't do anything worse, you found a way to do it."

"All we did was have Kyle dress up as a lunch lady," Dusty said.

Monkey Breath raised a bemused eyebrow. "Very good, Dusty. Do you know what you just did?"

Dusty shook his head.

"You just admitted that you and Wilson aided and abetted an attempt by Kyle to impersonate a lunch lady," Monkey Breath said. He pressed the intercom button on his phone. "Ms. Fortune, please come in."

A moment later the door opened, and Ms. Fortune entered carrying a pad of paper.

"A new rule, Ms. Fortune," Monkey Breath said. "From now on, any student caught impersonating a lunch lady — "

Ms. Fortune suddenly made a funny sound. It was sort of like a laugh masked by a cough. She quickly covered her face with her pad so that Monkey Breath wouldn't see what we saw — that she had a big grin on her lips.

Monkey Breath looked up at her and scowled. "Are you all right, Ms. Fortune?"

"Oh, yes." Ms. Fortune forced the smile away. "You were saying something about any student caught impersonating a lunch lady."

"Or any students caught aiding and abetting the impersonation of a lunch lady, will be punished by — " Our principal paused and rubbed his chin as if he couldn't decide what the punishment should be.

"One day of detention?" Wilson guessed.

Monkey Breath shook his head.

"Three days?" Dusty guessed.

Again our principal shook his head.

"A week?" I asked.

Monkey Breath shook his head. "Suspension."

28

The room went silent. I think we were all in shock. Even Ms. Fortune looked surprised. It was Wilson who finally broke the silence. "That really bites the hairy thingamabob."

"Yes," agreed Monkey Breath. "If that means what I think it does, then you are correct."

"Can I interrupt for a moment?" asked Ms. Fortune.

"Certainly," said Monkey Breath.

"I understand that the boys have broken these new rules," Ms. Fortune said. "And I understand that the punishment for breaking the rules is suspension. But strictly speaking, these new rules did not exist when Kyle dressed as a lunch lady and when Wilson and Dusty aided and abetted him in doing so."

"And your point?" asked Monkey Breath.

"That while these boys should certainly be punished in the future if they do anything like this again," Ms. Fortune said, "I'm not sure you can punish them now for something they did before the rule existed."

Monkey Breath blinked. His eyes began to glisten and pool. "What about illegal use of recording equipment on school property?"

"I will be glad to add that to the list of new rules as well," Ms. Fortune replied.

Principal Chump wiped something out of the corner of each eye. "Whose side are you on, Ms. Fortune?"

"I'm not on anyone's side," our assistant principal insisted. "I'm just stating a belief that it's wrong to punish a student for breaking a rule that didn't exist when he or she broke it."

"But those are the only rules they ever break!" Monkey Breath cried. You could see now that his eyes were definitely filling with tears.

Dusty turned to Wilson and me and mouthed the words *Going where no rule has gone before.*

Monkey Breath suddenly swung his chair around backward so that all we could see was the back of his head. "Out!" he shouted. "All of you! Out!"

My friends and I looked at Ms. Fortune. She motioned for us to follow her to the door. We jumped up and hurried out.

The door had hardly closed behind us when we heard a loud *crash!* followed by a pained shriek of *"Ahhhhhhhhhhhhh!"*

Around the office the secretaries winced and

turned away as if they were trying not to listen. Ms. Fortune pursed her lips and shook her head sadly. The banging and screams continued inside Monkey Breath's room.

"Know what, guys?" I whispered to my friends. "I think I just figured out what that soundproofing is for."

The next morning at the bus stop, Wilson had a big smile on his face.

"How come you weren't on the bus home yesterday?" I asked.

"Stayed after to work on our new movie," he answered with a yawn.

"When are we going to see it?" Dusty asked.

"You never know," Wilson replied with a mischievous grin.

I felt someone tug at my sleeve. It was Barfy. He'd left the dwarf pod and was holding out a York peppermint patty.

"Look at this," I said. "The single digits want to pay the bus stop tax even after we said they don't have to." I rubbed Barfy's head. "You're a good citizen, Barfy, but today you get to eat the tax yourself."

Barfy frowned and offered me the mint again.

"It's cool, Barfy," I said. "Seriously. You can keep it."

The next thing we knew the single digits surrounded us, holding up candy.

"What's this?" Wilson asked.

Not only were they offering us candy, but it was *good* stuff! Bags of M&M's, full-size Snickers bars, packs of licorice, and Sour Powers.

"I don't get it," Dusty said.

"It's a game to them," I realized. "They want to keep playing. Yesterday when we didn't take their candy, it must've really upset them."

"You mean, like, we didn't want to play anymore?" Wilson asked.

"Exactly," I said.

Dusty grinned and started grabbing the candy out of their little hands. "Okay, shrimps!" he growled. "That's better. And you'd better keep it up or else!"

Twittering excitedly and acting like they were totally terrified, the dwarf pod backed away.

The bus came, and we went to our regular seats in the back. A little while later, we stopped to pick up Melody. She sat down in the seat in front of us.

Wilson reached forward and tapped her on the shoulder. "I'd just like to say thanks."

Melody did a good job of pretending to be surprised. "For what?"

"That great acting job," Wilson said.

"I don't know what you're talking about," Melody said, but at the same time she winked.

We got to school and Wilson went down to the TV station. Dusty and I went into homeroom. Hart TV went on. As usual, it was the *Gary and Alice Show*, and everybody in homeroom began to talk and ignore them. Suddenly, the TV started to make staticky sounds, and Gary and Alice were replaced by a screen filled with greenish-gray snow.

"Now *that's* interesting," said Dusty.

"Yeah, it's a lot better than Gary and Alice," Cheech the Leech eagerly agreed.

Next, the scene cut to Gary and Melody standing beside Mr. Recycling Box.

"Wait a minute," Cheech said. "We just saw Gary in the studio. How could he be in the cafeteria?"

Dusty leaned over to me and whispered, "It's the tape from yesterday."

This time everyone in school got to see and hear Gary say how boring Alice was and how much better Hart TV would be if he were the star of the show.

The TV screen went all staticky again, and a moment later switched back live to the TV studio. Gary was sitting at the news desk with his mouth wide open, in shock. He looked pale, and his eyes darted this way and that. Alice was still sitting next to him, but she was glaring at him so angrily that you could almost see the daggers shooting out of her eyes.

The picture on the screen changed again. A title appeared:

THE BUTT OX BROTHERS PRESENT

THE TRUTH ABOUT LUNCH MONITORS

A MONKEY BUTT PRODUCTION
STARRING
BIG BERTHA AND WANDA THE WIDEBODY

The next thing we knew, we were watching Bertha and Wanda sitting at a lunch table in the empty cafeteria. Their trays were heaped with food, including two desserts each.

A voice-over began to play. It was a tape of Bertha and Wanda from the day they busted Wilson for eating dessert first.

"What'd he do?"

"Started his dessert before he finished his vegetables."

"You have to finish your vegetables!"

"That's a clear and intentional violation of the lunchroom rules!"

Meanwhile, on TV, Bertha and Wanda dug hungrily into their chocolate puddings and whipped creams. *Before* they touched any other part of their meals.

"Look at those hypocrites!" Cheech screeched. "They tell everyone not to eat dessert first, and then they go ahead and do it!"

Just in case someone hadn't been watching the

first time, Wilson played the whole segment again.

Finally, the scene on the TV cut back to the newsroom. Only now Alice was sitting alone at the news desk. Gary was gone.

"That's it for this morning's edition of Hart TV," Alice said with a stony expression on her face. "Please note that beginning immediately there is an opening on the news desk for a new cohost. Anyone who's interested can get in touch with me for an audition."

The TV went off. Dusty turned to me and grinned. "Looks like Gary just lost his job."

Suddenly, we heard shouting out in the hall. Ms. Taylor went to the door and looked out. A bunch of us followed her.

The Psycho Lunch Monitors from H.E.L.L. were stomping down the hall. Their faces were red and their hands were balled into fists. Monkey Breath followed them.

"Please don't go," he begged.

Bertha and Wanda ignored him.

"I've never been so humiliated!" Bertha grumbled.

"How can he possibly expect us to keep these children under control when he can't even do it?" Wanda wondered out loud.

"I'll try harder!" Monkey Breath swore. "I promise!"

Suddenly, Bertha and Wanda stopped and

turned. Monkey Breath fell to his knees before them and clasped his hands.

Wanda the Widebody gave him a look so withering it would have torn the bark off a tree. "Get a life, you wimp!"

Then she and Big Bertha stormed out of the school.

Except for Monkey Breath on his hands and knees, the hallway was empty. But every door was open, and half a dozen faces peeked out of each one.

Shaking and pale, Monkey Breath slowly rose to his feet and dusted off his knees. When he saw everyone staring at him, his eyes widened. *"What?"* he yelled. *"What are you all looking at? Go back into your rooms! Study! Read! Leave me alone!"*

The next thing we knew, he ran off down the hall and disappeared around the corner.

30

At lunch that day, my friends and I came out of the lunch line and headed for our old table. The cafeteria was crowded and noisy and filled with laughter.

"One question, Wilson," I said as we sat down. "How come you didn't play the tape of Alice dumping all her salads just so she could recycle the plastic?"

"I want to save that for when it could be more useful," Wilson answered. Dusty and I watched as he took a big spoonful of vanilla pudding and ate it before touching the rest of his lunch.

"Know what?" he said with a big smile. "They really have it backward. Dessert should *always* be eaten first."

"Think we could get Monkey Breath to make it an official rule?" I asked in jest.

"If you could find him," Dusty said. "I hear no one's seen him since this morning."

"Maybe he's in his room, breaking stuff and screaming," Wilson said.

"You know, there ought to be a rule against that," I said.

My friends and I grinned and clasped hands. "We go where no rules have gone before!"

Once again, the evil empire of Dr. Monkey Breath had been destroyed.

STUFF YOU CAN DO

Hi, this is Wilson Kriss. I'm Kyle's friend and the inventor of the Mouse-a-Pult and the Decrustifyer. Just between you and me, it's probably not a good idea to make a Decrustifyer, especially if it involves using knives or anything else with a sharp blade.

And if you want to dress up like a lunch lady, that's your business. But here are some things you can do without having the whole school think you're completely weird.

Bet the strongest kid in your grade that he can't sing "Mary Had a Little Lamb" while doing push-ups. You'll win. Bet him he can't fold a piece of paper in half ten times (no unfolding allowed). You'll win again.

Here's another one. Bet your friends they can't get up from a chair. Have them sit in a chair with no arms. They have to sit flat-footed with their backs straight, and they have to cross their arms in front of them. Now tell them to get up keeping their feet flat and without leaning forward.

And never forget that we live in a free country. No one can stop you from eating dessert first.

About the Author

Todd Strasser has written many award-winning novels for young and teenage readers. Among his best-known books are *Help! I'm Trapped in Obedience School* and *Help! I'm Trapped in Santa's Body*. His most recent books for Scholastic are *Help! I'm Trapped in My Lunch Lady's Body* and *Help! I'm Trapped in a Professional Wrestler's Body*.

The movie *Drive Me Crazy*, starring Melissa Joan Hart, was based on his novel *How I Created My Perfect Prom Date*.

Todd speaks frequently at schools about the craft of writing and conducts writing workshops for young people. He and his family live outside New York City with their yellow Labrador retriever, Mac.

You can find out more about Todd and his books at http://www.toddstrasser.com